For Mum and Dad
T.W.

This paperback edition published in 2006.
First published in Great Britain in 2005
by Boxer Books Limited.
www.boxerbooks.com

Text and illustrations copyright © 2005 Tom Willans

The rights of Tom Willans to be identified as the author
and illustrator of this work have been asserted by him
in accordance with the Copyright, Designs and Patents Act, 1988.

ISBN 0-9547373-7-7

Printed in China

Wait!

I Want to Tell You a Story

Tom Willans

Boxer Books

Once there was a muskrat
sitting quietly in a tree.

Along came a tiger.

"I'm going to eat you,
little muskrat,"
said the tiger.

"Wait!"

said the muskrat.
"I want to tell you a story."

"Okay," said the tiger,
"but make it quick!"

"Once upon a time,"
said the muskrat,
"there was a frog sitting by a pond.
A big shark came up through the
water and said, 'I'm going to eat you,
little frog.'"

"Wait!"

said the frog.
"I want to tell you a story."
"Okay," said the shark,
"but make it quick!"

"Once upon a time," said the frog, "there was a lizard sitting on a rock. A big snake came along and said, 'I'm going to eat you, little lizard.'"

"Wait!"
said the lizard.
"I want to tell you a story."

"Okay," said the snake,
"but make it quick!"

"Once upon a time," said the lizard,
"there was a fly sitting on a web.
A big spider came along and said,
'I'm going to eat you, little fly.'"

"Wait!"

said the fly.
"I want to tell you a story."
"I don't want to hear it!"
said the spider.
And the spider ate the fly.

"And I," said the tiger,
"am going to eat you, little muskrat."

"Wait!"

shouted the muskrat.
"There's more..."

"...the lizard ate the spider,

the snake ate the lizard,

the frog ate the snake,

and the shark ate the frog."

"What happened then?"
asked the tiger.

"The crocodile ate the tiger,"
said the muskrat.

"What crocodile?"

asked the tiger.

SNAP!

And the muskrat got away.

www.boxerbooks.com